BIG KID SCIENCE PRESENTS

Max's Ice Age Adventure

Logan Weinman
with Jeffrey Bennett

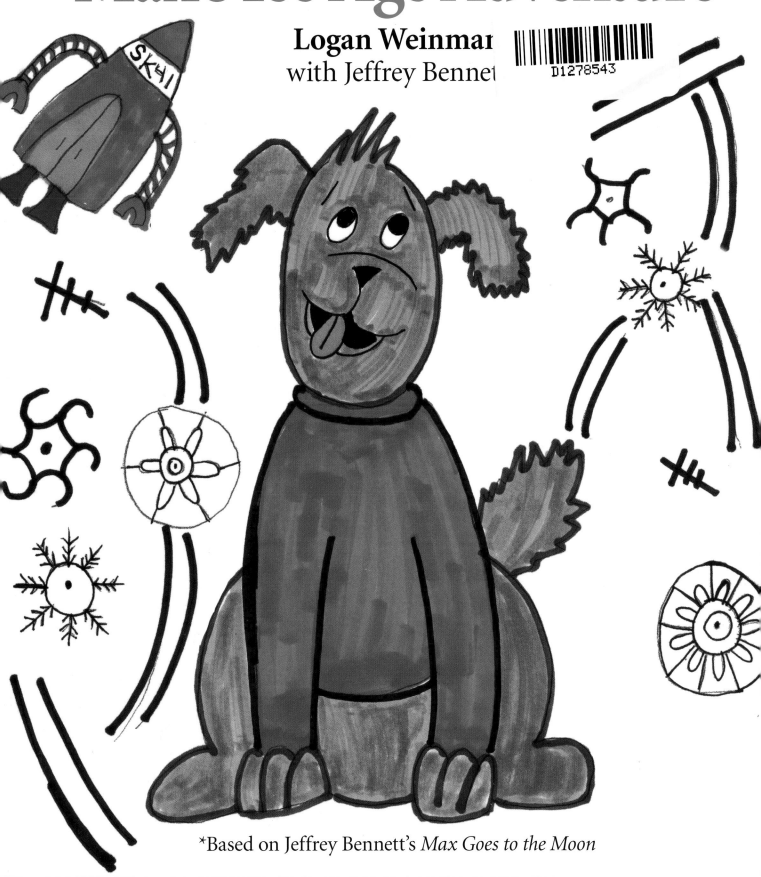

*Based on Jeffrey Bennett's *Max Goes to the Moon*

Also by Jeffrey Bennett:

For children:
  Max Goes to the Moon
  Max Goes to Mars
  Max Goes to Jupiter (coming soon)

For grownups:
  On the Cosmic Horizon
  Beyond UFOs (coming soon)

High school/college textbooks:
  The Cosmic Perspective
  The Essential Cosmic Perspective
  Life in the Universe
  Using and Understanding Mathematics
  Statistical Reasoning for Everyday Life

Editing: Joan Marsh
Design and Production: Mark Stuart Ong, Side By Side Studios

Published in the United States by
Big Kid Science
3015 Tenth Street
Boulder, Colorado 80304

ISBN 0-9721819-2-X

This is the story of how Max the dog and his friend Tori traveled to the time of the Ice Age—and brought home important lessons for our own time.

To children everywhere: I hope this book will inspire you to dream about your own science adventure. — JB

I would like to dedicate this book to my friends Lydia and Jeff for helping me put this book together and my Mom for helping with the illustrations. Also thank you to my Mom and Dad for their love and support. —LW

One morning, a group of
scientists were talking about
their greatest invention ever.
It was the Time Machine
"SK41."

Is time travel really possible?

No one knows, but it would certainly cause problems. For example, suppose you went back in time and accidentally prevented your parents from meeting. How could you then exist? Most scientists therefore doubt that time travel is possible. Of course, it's still fun to think about!

They were talking about who was going to test it out.
So far, no one had come to volunteer.

Just then, Max and his good
friend Tori showed up.

They immediately offered to test it out.

It turned out that they were going to the time of the Ice Age.

What is an "ice age"?

An "ice age" is a time when Earth is unusually cold. Earth has had many ice ages in the past, with some much colder than others. In fact, because even the North and South poles have been ice-free for most of Earth's history, we are in some sense still in an ice age today— although no one calls it that.

The scientists packed them up with self-assembling parkas (SAPs), especially one for Max, because he was so excited to go.

When everyone was cleared out of the way, Tori pulled the lever and they were off.

Although there have been many ice ages, when we speak of "the Ice Age" we usually mean the most recent cold period. This most recent Ice Age reached its peak about 20,000 years ago and ended about 10,000 years ago.

They experienced a mix of all kinds of colors as they traveled through time and space. It was a very beautiful sight, and a hint of what was to follow.

2006

Was Earth completely frozen?

No. The Ice Age was a time when temperatures everywhere were a few degrees colder and glaciers — sheets of ice that cover land and last year-round — covered much more land than they do today. Even so, the oceans remained mostly ice-free, and you would still have been quite warm if you visited a place near the equator.

Every little snowflake glistened as if it were jewelry. The Time Machine SK41 slid to a stop on the ice. Max and Tori set up camp for the night.

So where was it frozen?

During the Ice Age, ice extended much farther from the poles than it does today. For example, glaciers more than 1,000 feet (300 meters) thick covered most of Canada and the northern United States. Did you know that the Great Lakes were carved by glaciers from the Ice Age?

In the middle of the night, Max heard a noise, and started to bark.

What was out there?

Were there people during the Ice Age?

Yes, although Tori and Max don't run into any in this story. Ice Age people did not yet live in cities and probably survived by hunting and gathering food. Near the end of the Ice Age, scarcity of food may have been one reason that people invented agriculture.

Max and Tori looked all around but they didn't see anything in sight. So they went back to sleep.

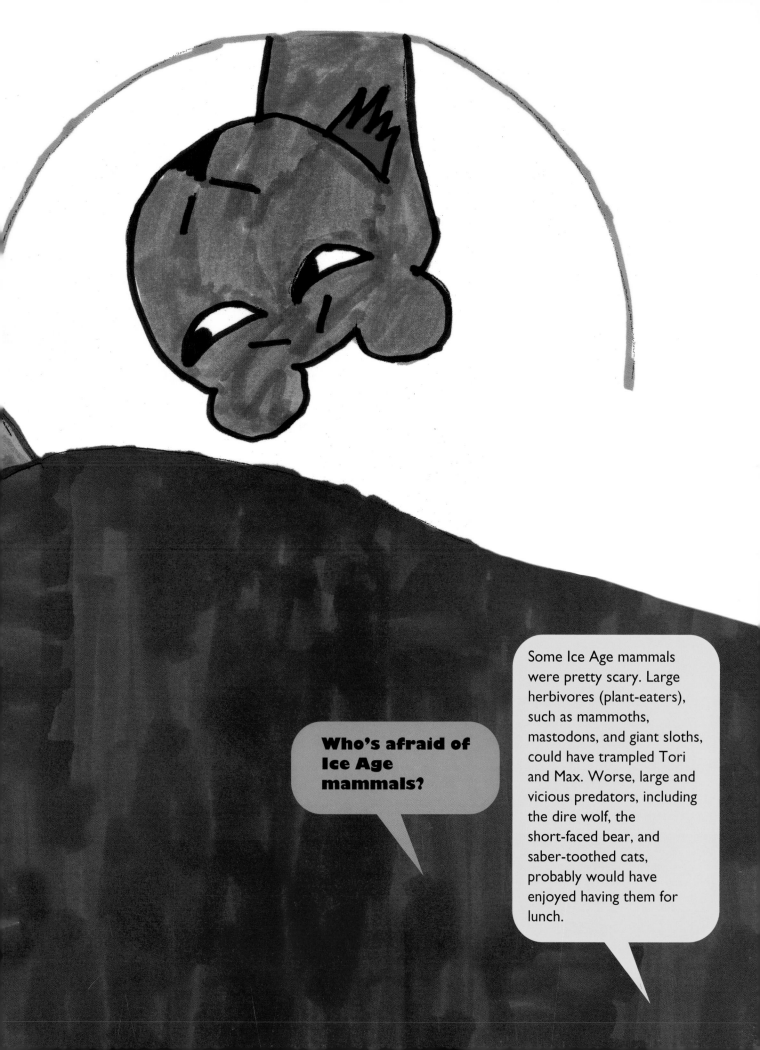

When they woke up in the morning, the first thing Max noticed was an ice cave with icicles above the entrance.

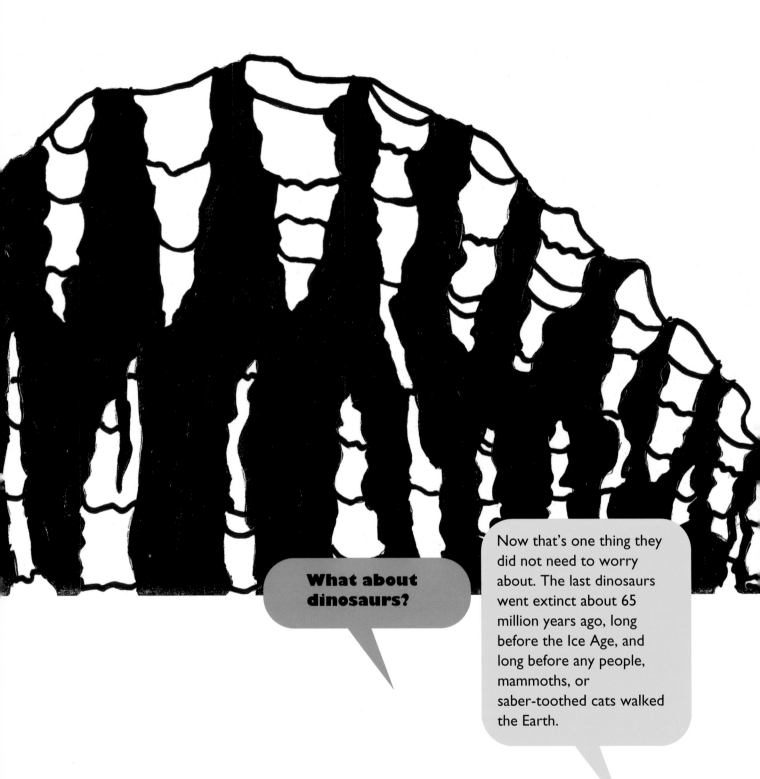

What about dinosaurs?

Now that's one thing they did not need to worry about. The last dinosaurs went extinct about 65 million years ago, long before the Ice Age, and long before any people, mammoths, or saber-toothed cats walked the Earth.

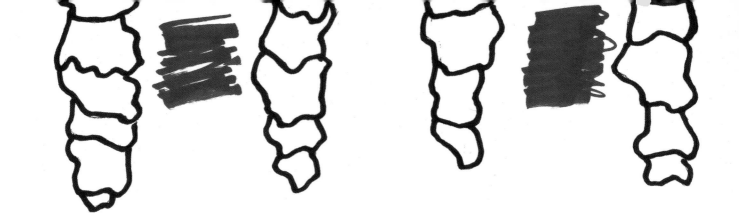

Max barked, and Tori immediately understood!
They turned around and saw. . .

. . . a saber-toothed tiger!

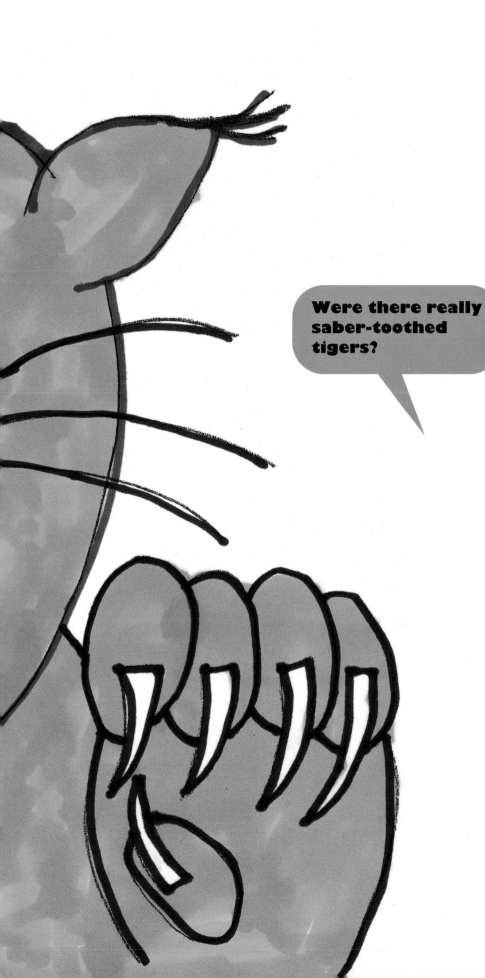

Were there really saber-toothed tigers?

The animals we usually call "saber-toothed tigers" were a type of cat, but they weren't tigers like those of today. In fact, there were several different kinds of saber-toothed cats. The largest, called *Smilodon populator,* grew bigger than Siberian tigers, which are the largest cats that exist today.

21

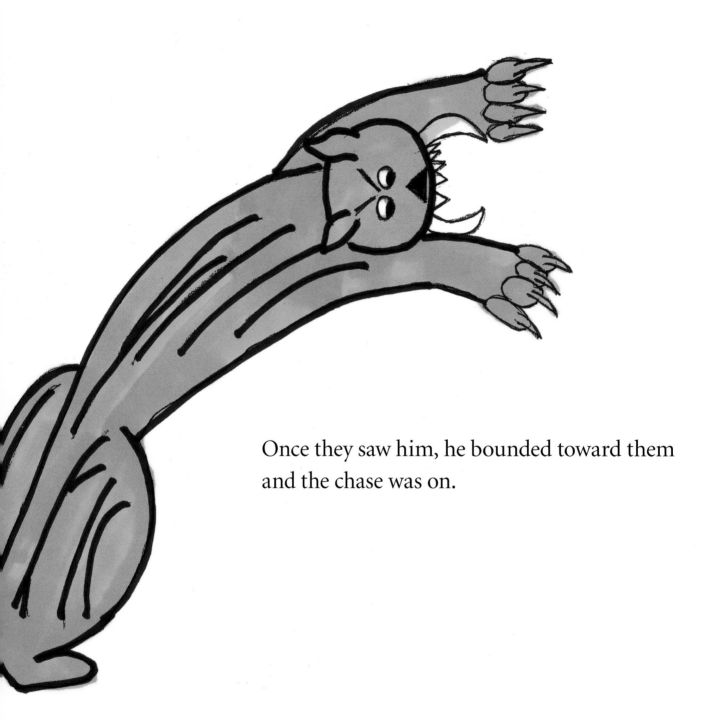

Once they saw him, he bounded toward them and the chase was on.

What are saber teeth?

The "saber teeth" are actually very long canine teeth. You also have canines — the two pointy teeth third from center (left and right) on the top and bottom of your mouth. You'll see sharper upper canines in dogs, wolves, and cats, and especially long ones in lions and tigers. Still, the saber-toothed cats had much larger upper canines than any animals alive today.

23

Tori and Max put their feet on the path of ice and they started to skate. They did flips, turns, dips, and dodges of all sorts.

What happened to the Ice Age mammals?

Many famous Ice Age mammals, including saber-toothed cats, mammoths, and mastodons, went extinct around the time the Ice Age ended. Some may have been hunted to extinction by people, but more were killed off by changes in the food supply as the climate warmed. Of course, not all Ice Age mammals died out. Most of the mammals that exist today — including human beings — were also around during the Ice Age.

Fortunately, the
saber-tooth tiger
eventually fell off
the trail.

Unfortunately, the sound of his crash started
a mix between an avalanche and an icicle
collapse. Tori and Max started going much
faster, until they finally saw the light of day.

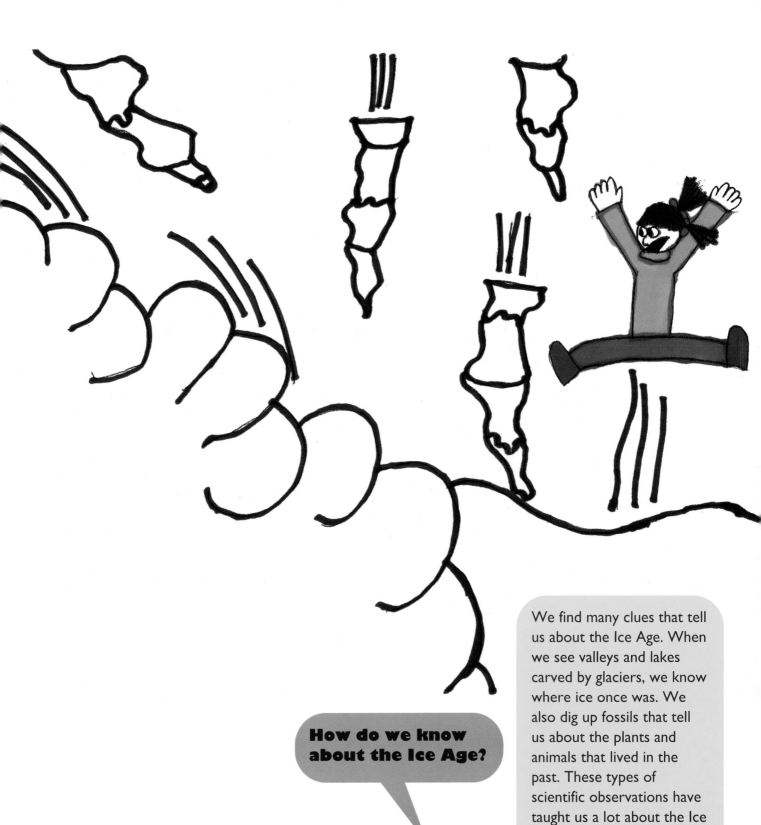

How do we know about the Ice Age?

We find many clues that tell us about the Ice Age. When we see valleys and lakes carved by glaciers, we know where ice once was. We also dig up fossils that tell us about the plants and animals that lived in the past. These types of scientific observations have taught us a lot about the Ice Age, though we still have much more to learn. Maybe *you* will someday discover something new about Earth's past.

Once out, they ran to the SK41 and pressed the
button to go home.

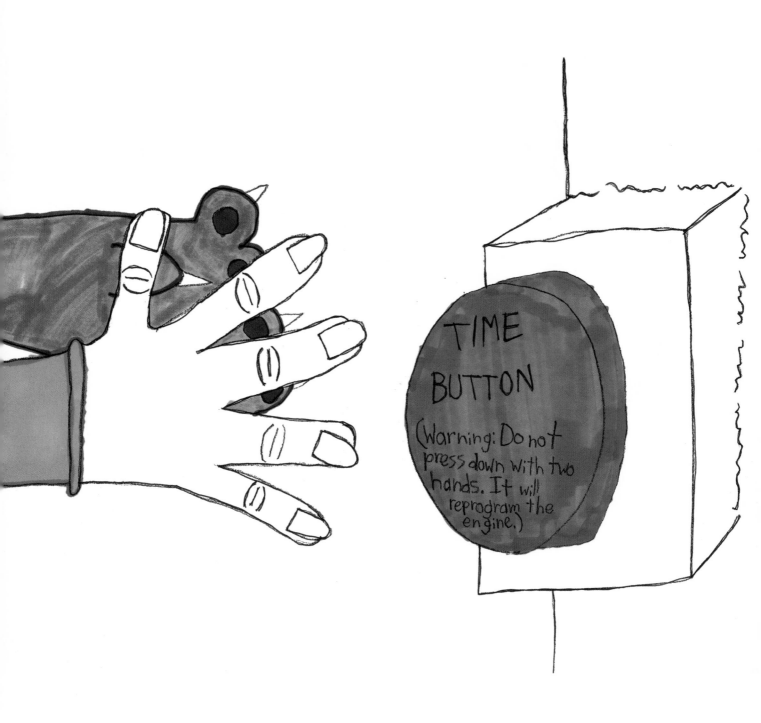

On the trip back, Tori wrote a report about what had happened and finished it just in time. Everyone around the world read it and everyone loved it.

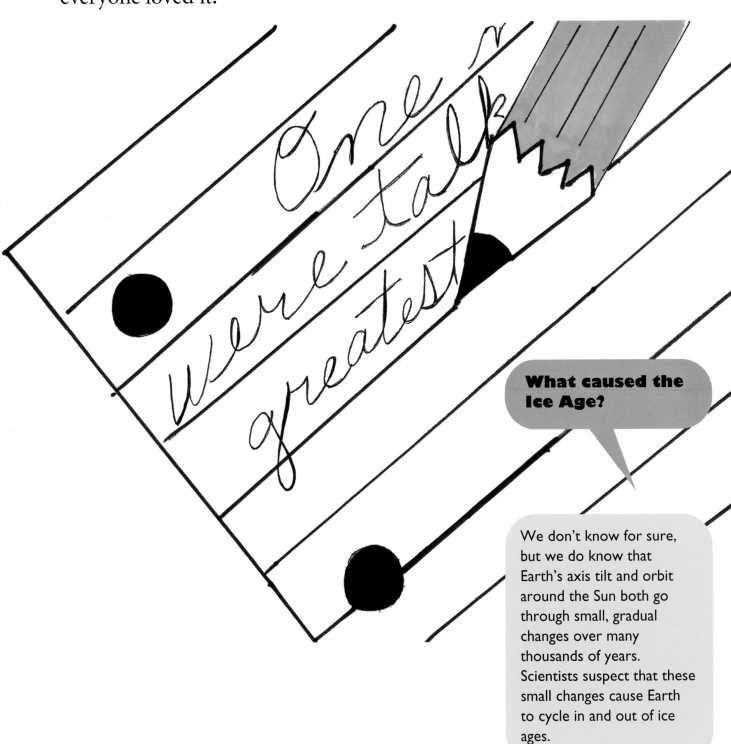

What caused the Ice Age?

We don't know for sure, but we do know that Earth's axis tilt and orbit around the Sun both go through small, gradual changes over many thousands of years. Scientists suspect that these small changes cause Earth to cycle in and out of ice ages.

And guess what? This book is that very report!
So pass the story on to someone who hasn't
heard it.